I0648247

Charles James

Joan of Arc

A Drama

Charles James

Joan of Arc
A Drama

ISBN/EAN: 9783337334277

Printed in Europe, USA, Canada, Australia, Japan

Cover: Foto ©Andreas Hilbeck / pixelio.de

More available books at **www.hansebooks.com**

JOAN OF ARC

A Drama

By
CHARLES JAMES

WASHINGTON, D. C.
THE NEALE COMPANY, PUBLISHERS
431 Eleventh Street N. W.
1899

Patron

JAMES R. KEENE

Dedicated

TO

FLORA RAYMOND

LIST OF ILLUSTRATIONS

PREFACE

JOAN OF ARC, warrior and saint, was so human as to be
almost divine. To her a war for wrong could be nothing but evil,
a war for right should be nothing but good : incongruous things
were not to her liking. She would smite the desolator, but once
overcome she would heal him. Good sense, courage and
constancy were her support, but grief and tears were ever by
her. Her purpose was direct, her decision prompt ; delay was
irksome to her.

The perseverance required to overcome obstacles she supplied
with unflagging ardor. Time was more precious to her than
rubies, and she made use of it with wonderful judgment and a
cheerful spirit. She was earnest before the altar, at council, in
the saddle.

On her arrival among the great Captains at Orleans she rated
the greatest of them for his unwise caution, and a few days later
she told him if he allowed the English forces to join without
forewarning her his head should answer for the default.

When a council of war, held without her knowledge,
determined not to fight she reversed its decision and led the
successful attack. She was not speaking or acting for herself,
but for a power she would not disregard. It required her to do
battle and she obeyed.

She furnished hope to the people, confidence to the army,
decision to the King, and in spite of court-craft placed the crown
on his head. Well did she calculate her strength; for her
allotted task once done her body began to sink under accumu-
lated resistance. King-craft and priest-craft destroyed it; but
her spirit broke through her prison bars again and again to

scatter her enemies, as it does now from her ashes to confound her detractors.

The Pucelle of Shakespeare's Henry VI. is not regarded as attaching to her. Voltaire aimed a shaft at her realistic excellence and it transfixed him. A ray from her transcendant life led Schiller into a labyrinth of supernal light where he followed the charming vision bereft of everything but his poetic genius and his passion to adore; and now sober historians crowd to the front with their chaplets, as did the companions of her childhood, and her veterans in arms, at her rehabilitation on the very spot where her body was consumed. Before he died the remembrance of her stirred even her indolent and ungrateful King to decided manifestations of manhood, and wrung from him the tribute — deserved, as Guizot says, "before God and men," — that to her more than to any and all others was due the ending of the Hundred Years War. The English historian, Green, says she is " the one pure figure which rises out of the greed, the lust, the selfishness, and the unbelief of the time," and this epitomizes the rest, as one who saw her on her charger wrote, " a thing wholly divine, whether to see or to hear."

This wonderful being first saw light among the shepherds of Domremy on the Meuse, on the 6th of January, 1412. In less than four years thereafter France suffered the humiliation of Agincourt and felt the iron hand of Henry of Monmouth, rapid and remorseless, closing on her vitals. Joan was bred amid the woes of her country; from every avenue they crowded on her vivid faculties. The grief they caused brought tears to her eyes and prayers to her lips. She regarded herself as an instrument of her Maker, but as weak and helpless, whose only power lay in the yearnings of a faithful heart. She could plead and did plead. She saw the Kingdom of France, fair and temporal, the Kingdom of Heaven, divine and eternal, and God as the Ruler of both, with a lieutenant for his earthly kingdom. This lieutenant she divined to be the Dauphin, and she saw him hindered and his trust fast going into the hands of a people who had come over the sea to despoil it. To avert this horror was the burden of her heart. Surely God could and would rescue his own if his own were worthy, and for this she prayed. She was cheerful at her vocations because duty required it, but this yearning never left her. But where was deliverance to come from? Human resistance had proved vain and France's enemies were doubling upon her; more than half the power of the Kingdom was against her. Her Dauphin, almost a fugitive, doubting his own legitimacy, would or could do nothing.

As the peril darkened she redoubled her appeals. Her zeal grew to a passion of anguish and supplication; then came visions. "St. Michael appeared to her in a flood of blinding light and bade her go and help the King and restore to him his realm." "Messire," answered the girl, "I am but a poor maiden, I know not how to ride to the wars, or to lead men at arms." "The arch-angel returned to give her courage, and to tell her of the pity there was in heaven for the fair realm of France. The girl wept and longed that the angels who had appeared to her would carry her away, but her mission was clear." Her time to act had come.

She left on her perilous journey of four hundred and fifty miles on the 23d of February, 1429. On the 9th of March she was admitted to an audience with the Dauphin; on the 28th of April she set out with her army for Orleans. On the 17th of July she caused the Dauphin to be crowned at Rheims, she, with her banner, standing by his side.

She regarded her task as finished, and with touching pathos entreated the King to let her go home; but he would not. Till then she had known no reverse in arms; but court-craft became more active against her and the energy she had infused into the weak King faded out. Even she could not rouse him. She continued the struggle with her accustomed bravery, but with varying success. She hurried to Compiègne on the 23d of May, 1430, and attempted to relieve the city by a sally which she led. The enemy rallied in overwhelming numbers and forced back her men. She covered the retreat, but the gate having been closed through fear, she and a few others were shut out. She struck to the last, and her words to those who spoke of retreating were : " Hold your peace ! Think only of falling upon them. It depends upon you to discomfit them." Similar words had been as a trumpet of fame in the mouth of the hero of Agincourt.

When called upon to yield, she replied, " I have pledged my faith to other than you and I will keep my oath." An archer came behind and dragged her from her horse. She was sold to John of Luxemburg, by him to the Duke of Burgundy, and by him to the English, who caused her to be burned by the Church as a witch, at Rouen, on the 30th of May, 1431. Other charges there were, but all centered in witchcraft. In war she had over-come the enemies of her country and, girl as she was, she must be a witch. By aggressive courage Henry V. at twenty-seven had almost miraculously won Agincourt, and he was England's hero. By singular bravery and address this girl of eighteen had discomfited his veterans, and she was France's sorceress. To use her own words she had caused her soldiers to " Fall upon them," when according to precedent and reason she should have led then in flight. The stake alone could atone for such obduracy. Joan believed in the Church, was, in fact, a child of the Church, and often during her persecution appealed to the Pope. But Rome was far away and the priests dare not heed her for fear of the English. She appealed firmly to God, and they gave her to Him through fire. " We are lost ! " said King Henry's secretary when the fiendish deed was accomplished, " we have burned a saint." " The English cause was indeed irretrievably lost," writes Green. The Maid had triumphed.

For a time all seemed hushed in the awful sanctity which guarded her memory; then the human conscience, an assize that knows no adjournment and is not hindered by any plead-ing, summoned the guilty to appear and answer her appeal. The Church was quick to disclaim the infamy and tear out the record; but unscathed and unheeding the Maid was already on her way down the ages, the genius of patriotism transfigured.

Joan of Arc had an overmastering love for her race and

country, an unselfish purpose, and an extreme desire to accomplish. Such a mind, if sufficiently intense, is liable to have visions, and they are liable to be angelic. They are the effusions of nature testifying to herself, of which the Maid is the rarest human example.

The following play aims at historic accuracy, and in no sense to depart from its spirit.

C. J.

Washington, D. C., 1899.

DRAMATIS PERSONÆ

THE DAUPHIN, *afterwards King Charles VII.*

GEORGE DE LA TREMOILLE, *the Dauphin's favorite.*

DUNOIS, *Bastard of Orleans,*

LA HIRE, *an Armagnac,*

ROBERT DE BAUDRICOURT, *Governor of Vaucouleurs,* } *French Captains.*

DUKE OF ALENCON,

PHILIP THE GOOD, *Duke of Burgundy.*

CAUCHON, *Bishop of Beauvais.*

THERON, *page to de Baudricourt.*

JACQUES D'ARC, *father of Joan.*

RIEL, *Joan's lover, afterwards made page to de Baudricourt.*

DUKE OF BEDFORD, *Regent of France.*

EARL OF SUFFOLK.

LORD JOHN TALBOT. } *English*

GLEDSTANE.

JOAN OF ARC.

QUEEN YOLANDE OF SICILY, *mother-in-law to the Dauphin.*

ISABEL OF BAVARIA, *mother of the Dauphin.*

MADAME ROMEE, *mother of Joan.*

Mother of Riel.

Uncle, Brother and Sister of Joan, peasants, citizens, a scullion, soldiers and attendants.

JOAN OF ARC

❦

ACT I.

Domremy.

Evening.   d'Arc cottage.   D'ARC, MADAME ROMEE,
Joan's Sister and Brother.

d'Arc.   [*Goes to the door and looks out.   To Joan's brother.*
   The night is threatening;
Have the sheep been gathered.

Br.   All that could be found,—a few are missing,
And there 's report Burgundians have been seen.

d'Arc.   So I have heard, but do not credit it,
Else we 'd been warned.

Sis.   Father Philip told us at church to keep close home.

d'Arc.   That comes more near.   Where is Joan?

Mme. R.   She 's gone to bed; all day she has been sewing
By my side, and went at once from supper.

d'Arc.   That 's a good report.
Will she attend our sports to-morrow?

Mme. R.   If the storm pass by she will.
I am to call her at cock-crow time.

d'Arc.   Indeed, 't is gladsome.
Seemed she in merry mood?

Mme. R.   Not merry, but cheerful.

d'Arc.   Why, then, her doubts may quickly pass away.

Mme. R. I question not they will. She said
It was the calmest day she 'd seen,
And that she felt a mighty change was coming.

            [*A muffled form passes the window. Sister watches it.*

d'Arc. Why should she take the Kingdom on herself,
A weak maid? God grant she may find rest.
Let 's all to bed and hope for a clear dawn
And that the Burgundian terror is a myth.

            [*Exeunt d'Arc and Mme. Romee.*

Sis. Look! where our sister goes — I fear 't is she.
She doth companion night, and woods, and dells.
This breeds distraction in her father's heart.
Oh, woo her from it. Have you not observed?

Bro. Oft have I noted her of late. Her life seems changed,
Disjoint and out of tune. Strange things she does, and in
Her eye kindles a glow like ecstasy.
How long has she been so?

Sis. Ever since the Burgundian youths o'ercame
Our village lads, and sent them bleeding home,
You with the rest, hath she been strange.

Bro. Why, that is four years since and more.

Sis. Yes. "In God's name!" she often will cry out,
Sleeping or waking, "had I been there it should not
Have been, but the Burgundians should have been
Discomfit." Then of a thought she 'll hie into the wood
And there remain for days, cheerful and safe
With birds and ravening beasts won by her gentle
Fearlessness and tact. From whence she will return
And ply her quiet work as if her wracking visions were a myth.
If her inveterate fancies leave her not
I fear some sad mischance may end her life.

Bro. Now may the heavens forfend.

            [*A knocking at the door.*

Who knocks so late? [*Voice. A friend.*
'T is Riel's voice. Come in!

            Enter RIEL.

So that you be not burdened with ill news,
You are a welcome guest.

   Riel. I know not what it is, I can not sleep. Wild rumors
Are afloat, and were I ominous, I 'd fear some lurking
Danger. For long I have not known so sorry a night.

                                  [Distant thunder.

Hark! how the thunder growls the sleeping hills,
As growls the mastiff rising from the hearth,
Doubtful if he 'll alarm the quiet house.
Nature seems ill at ease, and events,
Like actors, fret to hear their call.
Is Joan home?

   Sis. Her mother says she early went to bed.

   Riel. I could have sworn I saw her.

   Sis. Saw whom? Joan? When, where?

   Riel. As I came by the garden's outmost bound
A blaze of distant lightning cleared my view,
And ere the flash was burrowed in the clouds
A form like Joan's leaped the garden wall;
But when I called her name, what'er it was,
It sprang from bank to bank across the brook
And ran into the wood.

   Sis. This is our very fear. Go quick, my brother,
Seek first her chamber, then St. Margaret's glen,
There may you find her by the Druid's tree.   *[Exit brother.*

   Riel. Were my unguarded parents not my care,
I would remain until the event was proved;
For adoration with your sister dwells,
And in its train troop my most anxious thoughts.
But I 'll be early back to greet her here,
For peril has no shaft but she can turn and come safe off.

   Sis. Pray lend the time to tell how fared your suit
Before the Court at Toul where you appealed her
As your troth-plight wife.

   Riel. Like to a weakling's prayer, where there is naught,
For when in plain blunt phrase I told my tale,

And won the judges' minds, she, unabashed,
With an unblemished speech and graceful utterance,
Heeding the truth — not coloring her words —
Made me to feel I had no suit at all.
So swept she every doubt from her clear life
That all the judges wondering gave their voice
That she was not contract, and when she went
Amazement followed her.　Yet she protests
That but o'ermastering duty holds her back
She 'd leap with boundless love into my heart.
But here she curbs the scope of her discourse
And her unfathomed purpose blinds my hopes.

　Sis.　She 's deeply cloaked, but come to-morrow to our
Merry-make and, when all hearts are mellow
With delight, I 'll have her father ply her to the bans
Till she uncover or make good your wish.
She loves us all, and much she dotes on you,—
Of this I 'm sure.　Till then, farewell.　　　　　[*Exeunt.*

SCENE II.

Domremy.

*Midnight.　*JOAN* alone in the forest under the Druid's tree.*

　Joan.　I have great pity on the fair realm of France.
Her people have no King, but palpitate distressed,
A stricken flock, ravened by wolves;
Robbers from o'er the sea and her false children.
Her Dauphin, unannointed and uncrowned,
A fugitive in his own kingdom.
Were he proclaimed, the men might have stout hearts,
And meet the invader with prevailing arms.
This is her only cure, sick unto death,
A land of shrieks and moans.　　　　　[*Kneels.*

Oh, God! show France the way; her agony is mine.
Make her like to this Druid's oak,
With arms to shelter and to bless.
Sleeping or waking, I must pray for this,
Yearning so long, perplexed —
What is 't I see? It sure can not be day,
But now 't was midnight and the clouds were thick;
'T is dawning grace. See! See! the angels come
And look on me. Hark!   [*Listens.*
Poor misconceiving brain, 't was but a dream.
St. Michael, in a flood of blinding light,
Bids me to go and throne the Dauphin King.
I can not do it. I, a poor maiden,
Know not how to ride to the wars,
Or to lead men at arms —
Give France a mightier Captain.

Enter her Brother.

The light returns; again I see,
I hear. Oh, Blessed, take me with thee —
I can not leave France so,
Inconstant thought, Hark! —
He tells me of the pity there is in heaven
For the fair realm of France, and I am chosen
Of the Lord, our God, to lead the hosts,
And crown the Dauphin. These voices are of God.   [*Rises.*
I must go, my prayers are answered,
And my duty plain. Far liefer had I tend the flocks
And spin, but now I am heaven's messenger,
Armed with its power and destined to prevail — [*Sees her brother.*
My brother!
    Br. Joan, is this wholesome? Is it dutiful
To steal from thy safe couch into this wood,
Alone, where beasts abound, and worse than beasts,
On such a night, at such an hour, unguarded?

Joan.   Oh, sweet, my brother, rate me not so hard.
I 've been with angels, yea, with God himself;
Terror has fled and constancy rules here.
Though fears may shake, they are amenable.
Duty and Danger are my yoke-fellows.
Whence come you?

   Br.   From home.   We are not missed.   I found you gone
And sought you here.   To-morrow is a holiday, you know,
And all the youngsters gather at our house.
'T would grieve our father if you were not there,
Bright-faced and dutiful.   He dotes upon the time
Likely to be our last 'fore English manners
Shall usurp the land, and all that 's French forgotten.
Do not bereave us more, give o'er your wanderings,
Be to us Joan, not a mad gipsy, mumbling to the winds.
Come.

   Joan.   You read me ill, my brother, but I will,
The sky has cleared.   One day to dearest Domremy
I 'll give, the rest to France, whom God decrees
More holidays than one.

SCENE III.

Domremy.

Morning.   Enter JACQUES D'ARC *with* MADAME ROMEE, *his wife.*

   d'Arc.   The morn is wholesome.

Enter Villagers.

See, our friends are here.   [*To new-comers.*
Good morrow, neighbors,
Early stirring speaks a joyous day
For our time-honored custom.
It 's a fair month, and wisely chosen by our fathers
For troth-plight and for merry-making.
I hope the youngsters will enjoy the sport

And long continue it.   [*Sees Riel.*

Ah, Riel, it glads my heart to see you 'mongst
The first. A happy time we 'll have.

   Riel.   Joan 's not here.

   d'Arc.   That is our only cloud.

   Riel.   To me it 's midnight; nature 's in eclipse.

   d'Arc.   'T will soon dispel, for she has promised us,
And ever keeps her word. Her mother sought her
Ere the East was streaked and found her
In a happy state of mind.

Enter JOAN *with her Brother.*

See, here she comes
Upon her brother's arm, like a fair rosebud
Hanging from its stalk. Our flock is full;
Now, lambkins, to your sport.

       [*Riel and Joan converse while the others join in a dance.*

   d'Arc.   I hope, Joan, your merry heart is here;
This is betrothal day for your dear sister.

   Joan.   Oh yes, my father, here I see fair France,
As she shall be, as soon I hope she will be,
Redeemed from foreign yoke; then will I
Think of troth-plight with the rest.

   d'Arc.   Oh, my fair daughter, think of it to-day.
Dream not of France, God will preserve her
Ever, as He has.

   Joan.   Yes, of a truth He will, and that through me.

   All.   Through you?

   Joan.   Through me. I am his chosen war-chief,
And her guide, and by dread war
I 'll lead her to the light.

   d'Arc.   Your raving, girl, fills me top-full of grief.
Rather than so, I 'd drown you in the Meuse.

   Joan.   This grieves me, too. To filial duty
I was ever prone, and God first served,

So will I ever be.   To-morrow I will tell you what
I mean.   Your hint of marriage made me say so much —
I fear I 've marred the day.   Let 's say no more.

Enter a Peasant, excitedly.

Peas.   'T is Riel I seek.
Riel.   Here am I, sir ; your wish.
Peas.   I bring you dreadful news, but it craves haste.
Riel.   Quick, give it me ; more dreadful, more 's the need.
Peas.   Four false Burgundians have attacked your house ;
Your father 's murdered and your mother wronged ;
Even now the flames are bursting through the roof.
   Riel.   Oh, God ! the hell-hounds !
                    [*His mother staggers in, covered with wounds, and
                        falls into his arms.*
My mother !   [*They are assisted from the stage.*
                                    [*Exeunt all but Joan.*
   Joan.   Murder doth make each hour its own and slanders God ;
I must to my uncle, for he must be
The nether stepping stone to the
Dread eminence my hopes assail —
This cruel spur doth prick my maiden breast
To dare the worst that France may win the best !   [*Exit.*

SCENE IV.

d'Arc Cottage.

JOAN *descending from her chamber with a candle.*
The clock strikes three.

   Joan.   How quiet 't is !   Grief's clamors are hung up —
Fear's weary watch has cozened the spent night,
And makes a drowsy world !

The tired winds hang on the droning boughs, and the rank flood
Swells the far music of the shrill-tongued Meuse.
Ere the sun has silvered his dark face,
Or ere the lambs bleat up the willing ewes,
I should be gone. Oh Domremy! Domremy!
How am I tethered by thy cords of love!
Night-speeding memory be still awhile
Till I undo these fetters from my heart,
And, like the dove that homeless left the Ark,
Seek for the olive branch in War's wild storm.
How can I leave this fireside?
O maiden weakness! I am all too weak!
Here was I born; here Joy and Sorrow claimed me
In such terms as made my breast a shifting battlefield.
Here have I toiled in wholesome peasant ways,
Here have I joined in homely peasant sports,
And when all else have sought their restful beds
I 've sat beside my patient mother's knee,
Who, importuned, would stroke my willing head,
And tell me of the wondrous things she knew.
How wicked Pharaoh's host was swallowed up,
How high-souled Judith, Holofernes smote,
How Jepthah's daughter nobly gave her life,
How Deborah broke Jabin's hateful rule.
Thence, coming down to our all horrid wars:
How English Edward once laid claim to France
On some vague title of his ancestors,
And deluged it with French and English blood;
How Harry Monmouth then took up the strife
And piled up horrors till they broke the clouds;
And how his son, a little, puny boy,
Now claims the realm, while Bedford,
Talbot, Suffolk, and the rest
Herd misery in every Frenchman's home.
Sometimes a night-shriek hushed the dreadful tale,
When she would strain me to her bosom hard,

And with wide eyes hurry me off to bed,
Where I would hold my breath at every sound,
Till worn with watching I would fall asleep
To hear at dawn of crimes I dare not name,
Of ruined homes, pillage and butchery.
As I grew strong I wearied heaven for help
Till visions came to arm me for this hour,
Aye, and for many trials after this,
But this the greatest!
Far readier would I meet my country's foes,
Than the dear tyrants that oppose me here.
How they confound me as I tell them o'er:
My father's stern command, my mother's love,
My sister's pleading heart, my manly brother's grief —
These silent household gods! My lover's agony,
My church, my pastor and my loved companions,
Earth, sky, river, hills, flocks, birds and woods, —
All clamorous in one theme
As varying as a frantic lover's tale
Told in a hopeless maid's unwilling ear, —
Make protestations to my aching heart,
Till I 'm distressed if I be bond or free.
I 'm like a willow rooted in a bank
Which some mad torrent headlong leaps upon
To make contention with the wholesome earth,
Whether it go or stay!
They put my very vitals on the rack —
But hark! I hear my voices once again —
"Haste, Joan! Haste!" is ringing in mine ears.
Away these jailors, then; not all of these
A hundred times enforced can stay me now!
Quick, then, Oblivion, bring the tenderest robe
That ever duty fashioned in her loom,
Dyed in a halo caught from angel's smiles,
And wrap these jewel's from poor Joan's sight
Till France shall have a King!

Why, then, Farewell!
     [*Goes to each family portrait, saying farewell.*
There 's no farewell for me, but only pleading looks,
But yet, farewell! farewell! farewell to all!   [*Exit.*

SCENE V.

Vaucouleurs.

SIRE DE BAUDRICOURT, *Captain of Vaucouleurs, at his quarters writing.*

Enter THERON.

The. A man and maid desire to see you, sir.
de B. Admit them.

Enter JOAN *and her Uncle.*

Joan. [*Aside.*] Now comes the trial that shall try my heart
Whether I be a war-chief born or no.
Come, angel voices. France's buried Kings
Make convocation of her bleeding wounds,
Array her foes, unkennel every doubt —
Then set me in th' assembly of her wrongs
And put a pleading trumpet in my mouth
Till I fill full this soldier with a faith
That shall imbue the realm. How stern he looks —
Speak to him, Uncle.
 Uncle. Are you Sire de Baudricourt?
 de B. So am I called.
 Uncle. This is my kinswoman, she would speak with you.
 de B. What is your mission, girl?
 Joan. The Lord sends me to you, Sire de Baudricourt,
That you may take me to the gentle Dauphin

At Chinon, where I must go and have him crowned
At Rheims.

 de B. What crazy brain is this!

  [*To her Uncle.*] Did you not say she
Was of your kin?

 Uncle. She is my niece.

 de B. I charge you then to slap her soundly
And to send her home.   [*Turns to his table.*

 Joan. I must go see the Dauphin before Mid-Lent
If I have to wear my legs off to my knees.

 de B. [*Turning to her.*] And if you did go see him,
Then what would you do?

 Joan. Deliver Orleans and crown him King at Rheims.

 de B. Why, all the soldiers of his Kingdom can not do that.
How can a girl?

 Joan. No other can succor him save me.
I must go do it, for 't is my Lord's will.

 de B. Who is your Lord?

 Joan. God.

 de B. And who are you?

 Joan. Joan, a maid of Domremy, a shepherd's daughter.

 de B. Go tend your flocks. Shepherds
Should be peaceful. Women can not fight.

 Joan. A shepherd boy was braver than Saul's host,
And a fair woman once saved Israel from
Worse than Bedford's rule, or Talbot's arm.

 de B. If Jael you mean, when she slew Sisera,
He was asleep.

 Joan. But Deborah made Barak weary him, and so
Fulfilled her wholesome prophecy.

 de B. This Deborah had credit in the land.

 Joan. Faith comes of works as well as gratitude.
I must be doing.

 de B. There is no prophecy for you to work.

 Joan. A mighty one there is for me to fill.

 de B. Whose?

Joan. Merlin's.

de B. What is it?

Joan. From Lorraine's marches there shall come
A maid who 'll save the realm.

de B. When did you hear that?

Joan. From childhood.

de B. Yet you are but a child.

Joan. I am the maid who is to do that work.

de B. Your wit and courage, girl,
Might win a kingdom.

Joan. 'T is by hard blows we must strike off our yoke.

de B. Then men must fight it out,
Without God's help or yours.

Joan. The men must fight, God gives the victory.

de B. Then why not give it us at Agincourt?

Joan. King Henry was a scourge for France's sins.

de B. The priests told Henry that his cause was just.

Joan. That whetted him to do his dreadful work.

de B. And why not Bedford to continue it?

Joan. France now is humbled, and God pities her;
St. Louis and Charlemagne are on their knees,
And all the angels intercede for her.
By their assurance 't is, I come to you.

de B. Know you what war is?

Joan. With fear and horror it has chilled my blood;
But they have calmed each misbelieving doubt,
Making what 's hateful a necessity.

de B. And now you think it —

Joan. A dreadful instrument that must be used.

de B. Would you lead soldiers into battle?

Joan. There is no other way. 'T is not my choosing,
For it was I born.

de B. But fears are womanish.

Joan. Duty hath slain fear.
For France I dare meet Talbot arm to arm.

de B. He 'd feed the crows with you.

Joan. If he can take me, let him burn me straight.

de B. [*Aside.*] She would enamor men of war,
And coin weak soldiers into lightning shafts.
[*To Joan.*] Will you be my Captain?

Joan. 'T is by direction that I chose you first.

de B. [*Aside.*] She 's heaven-descended, beautiful,
And brave. Now will I prove if she be molded true.
[*To Joan.*] Have you ties at Domremy?

Joan. Father, mother, sister, brothers, lover, friends.

de B. Do you love them?

Joan. Better than life.

de B. And would you leave all?

Joan. Without leave-taking. It is my Lord's will.

de B. [*Goes to Joan and takes her by the hand.*]
      Brave girl, by God —

Joan. Swear not, gentle Captain, else can not
You be my soldier.

de B. Why, what can a French soldier do, unless he swears?

Joan. By your baton!

de B. Well, by my baton, then, I 'll take you
To the Dauphin, though robbers were as thick
As Vosges woods, and do believe
We 'll make the journey safe.

Joan. Fear not for that, gentle Captain, for I am sure.
                [*Goes to the table and picks up his sword.*]

de B. When shall we set on?

Joan. Better now than later; we must haste.

de B. Now be it, then. Have you a sword?

Joan. Not yet, gentle Captain, but the sword
Of St. Catherine is waiting for me
Behind the altar of St. Catherine-de-Fierbois.

de B. Until you come by that, keep mine;
It 's my best friend, as I 'll be yours
Forever after this.
[*To Theron.*] Get me another sword
And find a horse and armor for this Maid.

Joan.   Farewell, dear Uncle, and to Father, Mother,
Kin and Friends, say God be with them.

[*Exeunt all but Theron.*

The.   Ram's horns and Jericho!   Maids for captains,
Pinafores for shields!   My master is mad.
He has kissed every girl this side of the Meuse
For four leagues round, and here comes the prettiest
And he gives up his sword to her and makes her
His captain.   I will prig him a distaff for his sword.
He is as rattled as a dried mullen stalk.
—— What a trip we'll have through the woods
With the wolves, the bears, the robbers,
And the English, Oh, Oh, Oh!   [*Exit.*

ACT II.

SCENE I.

Forest, near Chinon.

Enter THERON.

The. I am Theron, the hunter; a brave hunter, I,
And what a hunt I 'm on, in search of war
And a kingdom, with a maid and two old Captains.
Was ever such a mad romp?
I 'm knock-kneed, ring-boned, spavined, hobbled.

> *My saddle 's bewrayed,*
> *My jerkin is frayed,*
> *And I am afraid,*
> *Following this maid.*

No rest, no peace, except when she sees
A church spire, she flies to it as if she
Were the first spring martin. I wonder where
On the map of the world Chinon is to be found?
I think we 've been three times round the earth.
I have n't heard a good, round, swelling oath
Since the moon quartered, and now she has quit
Night-walking. By my baton! swears La Hire,
By my baton! says my master, and the Maid laughs
And leads on. My master gives me the pleasant news
That to-night we are to be ambuscaded, and I
Am to be camp-watch. I think this maid
Must be a devil, to take in such a sinner
As old La Hire so easily. If ever
This Jason-meandering does crown the Dauphin,
He shall make me Constable of the Realm,

PAINTED BY W. ETTY, R.A.

FROM ENGRAV'D BY C. W. WASS

JOAN OF ARC

On finding in the Church of St. Catherine de Fierbois the sword she dreampt of, devotes herself and it to the service of God and her country.

Act II. Sc. I.

FROM AN ENGRAVING IN THE POSSESSION OF
THE CONGRESSIONAL LIBRARY

Or I 'll blow up his kingdom with a rush-light.
I am sent forward to find a camp. I wont stop at all —
Chinon or death ! That 's my motto.

Enter DE BAUDRICOURT *and* LA HIRE.

La H. Lord, Lord, I 'm weary ! Lugged with monotony !
All piety and no swearing. I have n't been in a fight
For a month. Where 's the Maid ?
   de B. At the altar, giving thanks for her sword.
   La H. I wonder if she 'll use it.
   de B. Take my word for it, she 's as eager as a hawk
After a moor-hen.
   La H. We are nearing Chinon, is n't there some way
We can spice this long tramp with a frolic ?
Where's your knave ?
   de B. Theron ? ·
   La H. Aye, that blank coward.
   de B. Sent forward to pitch the camp. I warned him
Of the threatened ambush.
   La H. Did you ? For fear that won't come off,
Let us play freebooters and scare him to death.
   de B. Not quite to death, but we'll abase the braggart.
Take you this cowl, I this, I found them in
The church.   [*They put on cowls.*
   La H. Monks or brigands, it 's all the same,
He will see horns, for he expects the devil.
Go you about and I will follow close.   [*Exeunt.*

Enter three Freebooters.

   1st F. Their man comes on, make sure of him,
And then its three to two.
   2nd F. Strike sure and quick that they do n't make us six,
For two such slashers do not live on earth.
   3rd F. Then there 's the Maid.

1st F. Fie, for the Maid, she 's at St. Catherine's shrine;
Besides, all maids fear ambushment like death.

3rd F. Fear it or not, she deftly holds her blade,
And in a close fight I would have her hence.

1st F. Here comes their man. Stand by and muzzle him.
If he do strive, slay him outright and quick. [*They stand aside.*

Enter THERON.

The. But two leagues more and I shall be at court.
I 'll summon the Dauphin and tell him I 'm the van
Of a new army that is coming to crown him.
My master can 't swear. If he raves
I 'll tell him I lost my way.   [*Freebooters seize him.*

1st. F. If you draw, you die; if you shout,
You shall guzzle your own blood !

The. I — I — I 'm a man of peace, a priest, a Palmer,
A prayer-man ; I 'll pray for you, Mr. Robber,
If you 'll spare me.

1st F. Give us your gold.

The. I have no gold, but two are coming with full purses;
I 'll go and lure them on.

1st F. With full scabbards, you mean, you scurvy knave.
                              [*Pushes him down.*
Lie there, nor stir, nor speak,
Or I 'll punch more holes in your gullet than
There are stops in a fife.   Here comes one of them.

Enter LA HIRE *and* DE BAUDRICOURT, *opposite.*

2nd F. And here the other.
Beshrew their monk robes, but I have a fear.

1st F. Upon them for your lives. They 're 'tired for heaven.

La H. And you for t' other place, and this of you.
On my French word, a fight and not a frolic.
This is fortune's rose. Come on, sirrah, and you —

We hunt in couples and have triplets found.

> [*They fight. La Hire kills two and de Baudricourt the other.*
> *In the melee Theron draws a cloak over him.*]

La H. Burgundians all, four sturdy cut-throats
Has good Philip lost, and we have not a scratch.

de B. What, downed you three whilst I bagged barely one?
I saw but only three.

La H. Neither did I ; but yet your score is two.
Mayhap you cleft your man, for here lie four
By very honest tale, and I did lull but two.

The. [*Peeping out.*] Your lullaby did prop my eyelids wide.
Are they all spooked ?

La H. My blade 's enraptured to keep up the tune,
Which is 't that babbles ?

The. [*Springing up.*] Don't, don't, don't, I 'm Theron,
The reserved corpse !

La H. [*Tearing off his cloak.*] Reserved for the gibbet.
Double shucked loon, why did you not strike ?

The. And deprive you? Oh, no ; I am too mannerly.
Chinon 's in sight.

La H. And so are you, thanks to these sober trunks.
Here comes our Captain.

Enter JOAN.

Joan. Are these men dead ?

La H. As yonder fallen elm. Punctured by us.

Joan. Why did you slay them ?

La H. To work our joints in trim for what 's to do.
They set on us, and missed, a chance affair, but trig.

Joan. And so went all unshrived ?

The. Oh no, for want of a better
I did that office for them ere they were carved.

La H. So did Judas for the Centurion's ears.
Let 's make Chinon. The sickle moon puts helmets
On its towers as if a conflict were agape for us.

Joan. Oh woful day, and many yet to come. [*Exeunt.*

SCENE II.

Chinon.

CHARLES, *the Dauphin, pacing his chamber in extreme grief, refusing
all admittance except La Tremoille.*

  Ch. Vain, treacherous title, empty gift of power,
Poor ceremony's fool, urn of frail joys,
Chamber of wretchedness, worse than a beggar's sty!
I know not if I am legitimate.
The English come like a consuming fire.
My soldiers fly like shadows from their path,
Or are pent up in fear.   France is o'errun;
Plunder is thrift, horror topples horror,
Hope is fled, ruin is king, and devastation
Shows such dreadful front that sudden death
Is craved for happiness, whilst I am
Self-imprisoned, but to wail.
Whence, then, Oh, whence can come deliverance?
I have heard it said a maid from Loraine
Should deliver France,—come, then, thou wonder!
If there's such a woman, for men seem helpless.

Enter a Page.

  Ch.   I will see none but George.
  P.   So I told the soldier, Sire.
  Ch.   What soldier?
  P.   Sire de Baudricourt from Vaucouleurs.
  Ch.   Of what sour news is he the messenger?
  P.   His mien belies him, if his news be sad.
  Ch.   Show me that prodigy, a cheerful man.
  P.   Nor is he cheerful, either.
  Ch.   Nor sad, nor cheerful?   Men seem splenetic,
Join in the death dance, fight, laugh over graves —
What seemed he like?

P.   One who knew his mind and came on weighty matters.

Enter TREMOILLE.

Tr.   Your Majesty,—
Ch.   First make me King, then call me Majesty.
Tr.   Sire,—
Ch.   Make France free, her King her choice,
And me that King, or hurl me headlong!
Tr.   My Lord,—
Ch.   Lord me no more.   I am like a sailor
Who has gone to sleep carousing 'mong mates,
And wakes confounded by the whirlpool.
Doubt and delirium is my estate,
The treasury 's empty, soldiers will not fight,
Bedford is coming on.   Canst thou add more?
Tr.   You may find sooth in what I have to say,
Though, I confess, I can not.
Ch.   Desperate is the cure, when the physician
Halts at his own medicine.
Tr.   It is not mine, Sire, but when he hears a groan
The quack is ready with his cataplasm.
Ch.   Approval is destruction, we lose at every throw;
Fortune will not compound with us, nor chance
Yoke up with opportunity to husband
What these eighty years have left, an English
Jungle for her slaughter-hunting mastiffs
Turned to wolves.   I 'll welcome any help,
Even magic arts.
Tr.   And near to that is offered to your hand—
Sire de Baudricourt and La Hire are fresh arrived
With a fair maid, who says she 'll save the realm.
Ch.   Whence come they?
Tr.   From the Meuse, and if she work on France
The change she has on them, you'd have to
Court her for acquaintanceship.

Ch.   La Hire is noted for blunt blasphemy,
The other is but freshly called to mind.

Tr.   He 's a rude soldier, but now both are tamed
And only ask to use their swords against the English
Under their new chief,— of other leaders they
Report the like.

Ch.   Your counsel?

Tr.   You know a woman upset paradise,
And that Queen Isabel —

Ch.   No more of that, are there no saints
To make a counterpoise?

Tr.   If you believe this maid, she is much more.
God is her Captain, saints are her lieutenants,
And those who follow are invincible.
'T is said the people troop her through the towns
And soldiers clamor for her.

Ch.   What say the priests?

Tr.   They all approve, save one, a youth
To whom she gave a biting answer.
She 's much in haste, and craves an audience
That she may go 'gainst Talbot at Orleans.

Ch.   Conduct her here at once; for such I 've prayed.
Haste me to see this wonder.

Tr.   So quick, my King, these are reports, merely;
I 'd put her to some test if they be true.

Ch.   Every fair trial fails, truth doubles like a hare
And reason is a baffled hunting hound, baying at fault;
Yet, it is so strange, there should be some proof.
What shall it be?

Tr.   She says tho' never seen she 'll know you at the first.
Put off your crown and mingle with the rest.

Ch.   And if she single me, I am resolved.
Call in the court, and then bring in the maid.

The Court assemble. TREMOILLE, *standing in the center, crowned;*
     BAUDRICOURT, *accompanied by* JOAN, *enters.*

Tr. Hearing the marvels that outsped your course,
How hope did drive distraction from your path,
To glad with smiles this wan and sickly land,
Famished and dying in the heated breath
Of grim invasion, your sovereign here,
With his assembled peers, will listen now
To what you can devise, or say, or do,
To drive this English curse from out the realm.
You have free audience ; freely then disclose.

   Joan. Your tongue o'erspeaks your station —
Crowns make not kings, else could a helmet
Make of me a chief. Yet chief I am and you are not
A king; were I in maid's dress, you in royal robes.
That rigol on your head, like an o'er hasty witness,
Spoils the tale. This stately presence doth enfringe
A prince and not a king. The crown of France
Is not now worn. Its owner is more circumspect.

                                        [*Kneeling to Dauphin.*

My liege !

   Ch. Who are you?

   Joan. A maid of Domremy, a shepherd's daughter.

   Ch. And who am I?

   Joan. You are the Dauphin, true heir to the crown.

   Ch. And what assurance do you bring of that?

   Joan. The voices of the saints that made me know you.

   Ch. The English possess Rheims, and promise soon
To take Orleans. Then how can I be crowned?

   Joan. They must be made to go home to their own country.

   Ch. How can this be done?

   Joan. By battle; body to body we must drive them hence.
Give me men at arms, few or many, and I will do it.
We must work fast, for I shall hardly last
More than a year. God wills this dreadful war
Shall have an end.

   Ch. Are you provided for this shock of arms?

   de B. Sire, she has nothing but a sword I gave her,

But she directed me behind an altar where I 'd find
A sword in waiting for her.   I went and found it
As she said, each word made good.   Here is the weapon.

                          [*Offering it to Charles.*

    Joan.   [*Springing forward and clasping it.*]   To me, to me,
This weapon is for me and hath a holy mission.

    Ch.   This doth confound all cavil.

    de B.   There is a mastery in all she does.
Robbers shrink back from ambushment,
And savage beasts are tame.
She throngs the street or church, wher'er she goes,
With wrapt beholders who do bless her steps.
Rude soldiers cease their oaths, and ruffian lust
Turns knightly honor in her radiance —
Past all conceit she is a leader born.

Enter Page with a letter for the Dauphin.

    P.   Sire, here 's a letter from the brave Dunois.
He bade the bearer fly with it.

    Ch.   [*After reading.*]   He, too, has heard of this deliverer,
And claims her speedy rescue for Orleans.
Whence comes this want?

    de B.   Sire, the courier winds do messenger her spirit
And speed a hope not known since Agincourt.

    Ch.   I am concluded.   Haste her to Orleans,
With all equipment that I can command —
Would that it match her worth.

    Joan.   We are enough if but our hearts are right.
Our present want is courage and a field.
What dare not Frenchmen when a girl shall lead,
What dare the English, seeing them so led.
Fear then shall trump her clangors in their ranks,
French valor shall look danger in the face.
Conquest shall pause, havoc and rapine
Shall go bootless home, and Monmouth's spirit

Shall go raging hence to see his conquest baffled
By a maid.   Now, quick decision wait on steady nerves
Till not an armed foe shall vex the realm.

SCENE III.

Orleans.

Enter JOAN *and* DUNOIS, *with forces meeting.*

Joan.   Are you the Bastard of Orleans, Dunois?
Du.   You 've called me rightly, and in you I see
Joan of Arc, Maid of Orleans hereafter to be known.
This famished city's been agaze for you.   [*Ringing of bells.*
Its bells now speak your welcome and its joy.
Joan.   It 's a dear greeting, I have ever loved them.
We crossed the Loire and came by the south bank.
Was 't by your counsel?   It was my wish
To keep the north and startle war-like Talbot
With a call; as we have business, it were best
We meet; when we have cured him of his slaughtering
Trade, belike we 'll have this Godden home to dine.
Du.   Our oldest and best Captains advised otherwise,
Else had their bastiles swarmed like angry bees
And stung you ere we had you.
Joan.   Your fears deceived you.   They dare not budge,
An' if they dare, Orleans had now been free.
My warriors are in trim, confessed and true.
I bring you the best succor ever sent,
An earnest soul and God's prevailing spirit.
— Have you ink and paper?
Du.   Both, and at your service.
Joan.   Write what I say; bid Talbot, in my name,
To take himself and men to his own country,

And void this strife which, as he 's English,
He has cause to fear, and if he 's Christian
He should strive to shun.   Dispatch the message
And be ready to fall on, or mingle friends,
At Talbot's yea or nay,— all 's now with him.   [*Exeunt.*

SCENE IV.

English Camp.

Enter TALBOT *and* SUFFOLK.

Tal.   There is a mighty stir among the French.
Huzzas, bells, guns, and music shake the air,
While flags new dress the city.
Is it submission, or some victory ?
   Suff.   I can not tell, but yesterday Dunois
Sent me a mantle rich with compliments ;
I thought it prelude to a friendly parle.
   Tal.   Pray God his present prove him not a Greek,
Nor I a Priam waked to a lost Troy —
For through the watches of a restless night
I dreamed of challenge, sally and assault,
Of broken squadrons and dismantled forts,—
The appalling shapes of changeful, sickening war.
What think'st of this ?
   Suff.   It may be evil portent.
   Tal.   Why, we are proof, let evil do its worst;
The power to shatter England is not nursed.

Enter GLEDSTANE, *with two French Messengers.*

   Gled.   [*Addressing Talbot.*]   My Lord, as I was coming up the
Hard by the farthest bridge, a host of French   [Loire,

Swarmed up the southern bank under a leader
That I had not seen, with martial tread,
And filed into the town, whence there arose a shout
Would tax a realm ; flags were displayed, spires pealed,
And cannon roared. Nearer to you I came upon
Two Caitiffs with a white flag, who said
They bore you missive from the Maid, a holy girl,
Whom God had sent to help the Frenchmen out.
Some trull, no doubt, is bantering with their hopes,
And, as they dare not meet us in the field,
Their dernier is this incantation trick.
I 'd hang the mendicants and scourge the jade.
These are the vagabonds. [*The messengers hand Talbot a paper.*

 Tal. [*Looking at paper.*] This shows you good at divination,
Gledstane. Dunois has lost his wits, the proof I 'll read.
[*Reads.*] " To Talbot, Christian, you call yourself,
"And Englishman: In God's name I charge you go home,
" Or I will beat you hence with blows."
Signed " Joan, the Maid," with a cross.

 Gled. I 'll be her partner in this mawling match,
And slash her face with crosses that will last.
Give me the front.

 Tal. Why, so we will ; secure these wretches ; arm at once ;
Send her defiance in what terms you will,
We 'll give this jubilee an English face.

 Gled. My lord, I 've done your bidding ere 't was bid.
Defiance have I shouted o'er their walls.
Now will I make the canting harlot blush
Ere death shall claim her crimsoned on my blade. [*Exit.*

 Tal. Men have gone mad, and if this buffet holds,
Henry will have a realm of lunatics.

 Suff. This latest turn is stranger than a dream ;
I marvel it may finish up the play.

 Tal. God grant we then may have a lasting peace.
Oh, Suffolk, it doth weary me to think
On what a slender pivot men will fight,

Tripping with carnage o'er death's border line.
Pale, jostling shades gasping equivocation.
A fool could jest at it; for take a soldier's word,
That proud contention is a braggart's breath
As vapid as a witling's vagrant looks
Gaping at space.
Why should we war on France, or France on us,
For that glint shadow, vain authority,
Whose mantle now is Harry Monmouth's robes
And now his shroud indifferent.
Earth has no unborn horror, and 't is meet
That hell should ope its jaws
And make this strife infernal.

    Suff. My lord, methinks you conjure with effect,
There is a rumbling shakes the solid earth.

    Tal. It 's like the rush of battle.
Nearer it comes, as if the foe, insane,
Had left their walls.

    Suff. That would enthrone amazement, scare the age.
Startled oblivion would not more stare
Than our roused soldiers at a dare like that.

    Tal. Sound has turned false, or they are at our tents,
And witch-brewn valor is enacting war.

Enter a Messenger.

    Mess. My lord, hard by the French have taken a redoubt
Hotly contested ; Gledstane is down ; your front 's
O 'erthrown ; a maid in triumph storms your flying camp.

    Tal. Out, hell mouth,— voice of the devil's dam,
Lime of the fiend ; thou whiff of gibbering fear,
That wouldst infect a host. Your English tongue
Speeds bickering witches' rune.
Hath hell no sorrier throat than thine to croak ?
Were 't but thy mouthing I would not believe thee.
Out I say.   [*Exit Mess.*

[*Aside.*] If it 's truth, we must out-face the truth,
These chasing wonders make my hair stand up.
[*To Suff.*] My lord, let 's blast this phantom ere it fangs.
  Suff. I 'll play Achilles to this Amazon,
And if she shrink not from my courtesy,
I 'll bring her for a show. [*Exeunt.*

SCENE V.

Joan, with soldiers at a barred gate.

Enter Dunois.

Joan. Fair Count, we 're prisoners and not a blow.
Du. How! prisoners?
Joan. Yes, prisoners by the French.
We came to fight, and marched into a prison.
Fear 's in command. The gates are barred.
We are all mewed up. Sheep in a fold are not less dangerous.
  Du. Our captains counseled but a brief delay.
  Joan. A brief delay may cause a heavy reckoning.
My counsel 's different.
Know you not Falstoff 's on the move?
Dunois, Dunois, if he join Talbot,
Save in Talbot's flight,
The event may slice off your unwary head.

Enter a Soldier.

Sol. Brave Count, Talbot detains your messengers
And sends back an ugly defiance.
  Joan. As I rode 'round the walls 't was howled at me
From Gledstane's vulgar throat —
Oh, how I pity him, so near his end.

These English mastiffs growl our very doors.
Let 's show them lions where they looked for sheep.
Loose us, fair Count, and we will after them.
   Du. You 're in command.
   Joan. Break down the gates!   [*Soldiers break through.*
Now, will La Hire, Alencon, and myself, with
Our small power, show you how nimbly
Englishmen can skip. This will be a great day
For France and for the King.
Forward, then, though they were hung to the clouds
We should have them.   [*Exeunt and din of battle.*

[*Curtain rises. The French, led by* JOAN, *storming a fort. She places a ladder to the wall, mounts, is pierced through the shoulder with an arrow, falls. The English rush out to seize her; she is rescued; plucks out the arrow and renews the attack. The French follow her into the fort; drive out the English, when she appears upon the walls, surrounded by the French, and displays her banner. Curtain veils them.*]

Enter THERON.

   The. Tear forts to flinders, scale walls, topple towers,
Blow trumpets till they split.   It 's a hot fight.
The blows I have struck to-day would sack Rome.
My blade hath such a sweep I make no captives.
The Maid and I were neck and neck after them.
" Fall on!" she cried, and flew up a scaling ladder
Like a hobby after a sparrow.   An arrow
Sent her headlong, like a duck into a pond.
Who falls on may fall off.   That 's the bit
That curbs me. When she was down I faced a legion
To defend her, then in bounced La Hire hand and foot
And spoiled my play — the frothy brigand.
He 's a callet coster, and fights as he prays,
With his tongue. Her banner 's flying, though.

It comes this way.   An Ajax dimness blinds me.
I 'll fall off whole to clear my sight and breathe,
But when I charge again, God help old Talbot.
Here he comes.   [*Runs off.*

Enter DUNOIS *and* LA HIRE.

Du.   The Maid is wounded, we must now retire.
Enough of glory has she won to-day,
Enough for her, for France and for us all.

Enter JOAN.

Joan.   Who says retire?   I pray you, let the English
Have that word, and wear it out in flying
From the French.   My wound is but a tell-tale
Of our work.   In God's name! we must fight them.
It 's their last hold.   Oh, my brave soldier,
Say Onward! rather, till we see their backs,
For when my banner doth caress their walls,
Then mount and all is ours.
   La H.   Onward! I say, fair Count, whate'er betide;
When she says Onward, I am at her side.
   Du.   Why, so am I.
   Joan.   Why, then the fight is won.
Orleans is free before the set of sun.   [*Exeunt.*

Enter TALBOT *and* SUFFOLK.

Tal.   The fiend is down, now England ply your work.
   Suff.   She 's up again, my lord, and at our walls.
Five forts she 's taken, and now storms on this.
   Tal.   A murrain seize her! we will drive her hence,
And win them back again, or English Talbot
And our English arms have lost the glory
They have won in France.   [*Exeunt.*

Enter THERON, *running across the stage, followed by* JOAN *and*
SUFFOLK.

Joan.   Thou 'rt not dread Talbot whom I dared afield ;
Tell who thou art that call'st on me to yield.
    Suff.   I am the Earl of Suffolk, and have sworn
To make thee captive, or as captive mourn.
    Joan.   Then quick, lay on and let our swords debate,
For by no words can I be captivate.
               [*They fight.   Joan wounds and disarms him and he flees.*

Enter DUNOIS *and* LA HIRE.   *A host seen flying pell mell across a*
bridge in the distance ; bridge falls.

    Joan.   They fly ! they fly !   See swift Alencon drive them
O'er the bridge.   Look !   Look !   Heaven's mercy, it falls.
Oh, God, they are unconfessed and overwhelmed,
Wild consternation doth possess their ranks,
And every hold is ours.   Now, noble Count,
We will retire, as soldiers should, and beam our
Victory on the grateful town, where looks, not words,
Shall be our messengers.   Give thanks to God
And glad the Dauphin's heart.
    Du.   Here on this field, I 'll speak ; my heart is full.
You have this day o'er topped all feats of arms,
And won a title mightier than a King's,
Maid of Orleans, forever to be known.
    La H.   I say amen to that.
    Joan.   Call me to duty by what name you will,
But now let 's visit the delivered town
Which had no welcome for its English guests,
And see what cheer 't will give the weary French.   [*Exeunt.*

Re-enter THERON, *leading a camp scullion by a rope.*

    The.   We 've whipped the English, Talbot is paid.

I cracked his crown, and sent him flying
Like a clipped widgeon, with La Hire after him,
While I rummaged his camp. It was as empty as a
Dried herring box, except this luggage, which I found
Stowed in a sour wine cask. I scaled his fort and
Brought him out by the ears. Art thou some Knight,
Or Lord, chalking, like David, on the gate to baffle me
Of my ransom? Shall I not be enriched of thee?
Go thou before, thou ghost of Harry Monmouth, step proud,
That my capture may show fair. Why, you chatter like
An old church weather-vane in a gale, and wink like
The fag of a baboon hunt. What art thou?
Speak, if fear have not leavened thee.
   Scull. I belong to the kitchen service.
   The. The kitchen service! Get behind me, thou imp
Of submission, thou slave of forty conquerors.
I'll go before. Victory beats in my breast
Like a town bell. Hurrah! The Maid and I will crown
The Dauphin. It is our destiny, we were born for it.
Come along, thou residuum of a defunct camp, thou
Elaborate unity of mustiness, thou jackal of Bacchus'
Laboratory, thou pan-holder to Lucifer's pot wench,
Come along. I weary of abatement and long for
Another grapple with the enemy.   [*Exit.*

SCENE VI.

A street in Orleans.

Enter Citizens.

   1st C. Orleans is saved!
   All. Hurrah, hurrah, hurrah!
   1st C. And now we'll have our own French King.
God bless the Maid!

2nd C. I saw her place a ladder to the wall
And mount the first.

3rd C. The English fled like hares, or fell in heaps.

1st C. Oh, but the French were brave,
They held the Maid in chase as she led on.
'T is said she vanquished Suffolk arm to arm.

2nd C. I saw them meet. There was a blaze of steel,
And then he fled.

1st C. Oh, grand deliverance!
Here come the victors back;   [*Joan and soldiers pass.*
How proud Dunois is, riding by her side;
He has new christened her, "Maid of Orleans."

2nd C. 'T will buckle to her while there is a name,
And fame him god-father,
While there's christening.
— See, they dismount and enter in the church.

3rd C. Let's all go in.   [*Exeunt.*

SCENE VII.

Orleans.

Battlefield.   Night.

Enter RIEL.

Riel. She comes this way. I will lie here to guard her
While she prays.   [*Lies down, the moon shining in his face.*

Enter THERON.

The. My master bade me watch and guard her,
I'll hide me here behind this fellow
Whom I slew. Ugh, he looks like Cerberus

Guarding the pit.   Thou 'lt rise no more,
Thy valiant spirit have I quenched in night.
                              [*Lies down behind Riel.*

Enter JOAN.

Joan.   Oh, how these tears start streaming from my eyes
As my sad sight beholds these slaughtered men.
The moon looks down cold as the damps that bathe
Their rigid brows.   Some French, more English,
But I mourn them all.   Oh, Talbot! Talbot!
Why didst thou come on to drive a people
Desperate with woes, whom God would rescue!
                              [*Kneels, gazing at Riel.*

Enter TALBOT.

Tal.   Some one called me.   Gledstane, perhaps,
Dying and alone—   [*Sees Joan.*]   A woman!
Kneeling, angel must she be.
   Joan.   [*Rising.*]   Who goes there?
   Tal.   An Englishman.
                  [*Riel half rises; Theron springs up, falls, runs away.*
   Joan.   Come, then, and weep with me this English work.
   Tal.   This is no English work, they are the slain.
   Joan.   The prowling hunter who doth seek her whelps,
Slain by the lioness, but slays himself.
   Tal.   England but claims her own, this Kingdom
By solemn treaty granted.
   Joan.   That was the treaty of an insane king,
And 't is insanity to sanction it.
   Tal.   The Dauphin's mother gave her name to it.
   Joan.   She 's alien to France's welfare as her blood.
   Tal.   But for the witch the French would soon submit.
   Joan.   What witch?
   Tal.   Joan of Arc.

Joan.   I tell thee, Englishman, she is no witch,
But sent of God to drive the English home.
I am Joan of Arc, here, weeping for these slain.
Is this a witch's work?
 Tal.   And I am Talbot, who will strike thee dead.
       [Riel rises, lays his hand on his sword.
 Joan.   On thy soul's peril, no.   This sanctity
Is stronger than thine arm, that shunned
To meet me when I challenged it;
Kneel here and ask God's grace, that ever thou
Didst make this slaughter-house.
Yours is the work, on your soul is the sin.
 Tal.   Whate'er you be, you 've called me to my wits
Which I had near o'er-run.   John Talbot
Will not strike a woman on mercy bent
And praying here alone; his arm is nerveless
In such a quarrel.
 Joan.   And nerveless be it then in Henry's wrong.
Oh, turn it rather 'gainst the infidel,
And I will be your soldier.
I warn thee, Talbot, but that you relent
You'll be an humble captive to my King
Suing for ransom.
 Tal.   Before that, I 'll sell my bones to kites.
 Joan.   Here is a feast for kites prepared by you.
Is 't not enough?   These men should have gone whole
To tears of joy for streams of hopeless grief.
 Tal.   'Till this, I ne'er turned back upon a field.
 Joan.   Nor never would in any rightful cause.
 Tal.   You 'd fill me full of treason to my King.
 Joan.   I 'd fill you full of blessings to two realms.
 Tal.   *[Aside.]*   At every turn I make she baffles me.
Whether she 's saint or devil, I am tamed.
She woos me like a templar to her cause;
Then shatters mine as Nathan shattered David.
[To Joan.]   Joan, I leave this field to you.

Joan. Better have left it me before 't was fought,
Now shun the shame I have foretold of you. [*Exit Talbot.*
Now for the King, to make him all a King. [*Exit.*

SCENE VIII.

A Street in Rheims.

Enter Citizens.

1st C. The Dauphin 's coming to be crowned. Stand close.
2nd C. Does the Maid come with him?
3rd C. She goes before.
1st C. Why is her banner borne before the rest?
3rd C. 'T was foremost in danger, therefore 't is first here.
2nd C. Was ever such a woman?
1st C. Yes; Esther, the Queen.
3rd C. She was not. She got Vashti's place
Because Vashti would not junket
With the King and his lords.
1st C. Tush! these are holy matters. That is Tremoille,
The Dauphin's favorite, who doubts the Maid
And seeks her overthrow. Next him is Dunois,
And next Alencon.
2nd C. Who 's that grim soldier that brings up the rear?
3rd C. That is La Hire, the Armagnac.
2nd C. Does he doubt the Maid?
3rd C. His sword is out if any doubt her.
Hark to the music — [*A pause. Solemn music,— ceases.*
They 've crowned the King.
See, here he comes behind the holy Maid.
  [*King and train pass. Exeunt citizens.*

Enter THERON.

The. Here 's a fine jolt of fortune's wheel,
While I was oiling it. The Dauphin 's crowned,

Whilst I am unhorsed, upset, ditched and abandoned
Like a broken cart, and all because I oracled
After the court pet about the Maid, and said
She was no great of a Captain after all;
Whereon a fellow hit me over the head a blow
That set every cerebral octave piping like
A church organ. He said I lied in my throat
And was, moreover, a coward. At this I would have
Felled him, but I saw he was the same chap
That rose from the dead on the battlefield
At Orleans where I slew him, one who won't stay killed.
He taxed me with running away, too,
And leaving the Maid. Good time to run
When the dead leap. My master, hearing the quarrel,
Sent me adrift and took him. That's the reward
Of success; winning a kingdom on small means.
I 've been the rear guard of every attack,
And the herald of every victory since we left
The Meuse. I 've taken but one captive alive,
And him I sold to a barber for half a franc.
There 's no profit in war here; Alexander the Great
Would become a parish charge at it. The land
Is looted as bare as a priest's Sunday face,
So I 'll to the road
> And in the closing of some dreadful day
> I 'll take a purse, or else I 'll run away.

SCENE IX.

Rheims.

Enter KING, QUEEN YOLANDE, *Court and* JOAN.

K. Fair lords, and gentlemen, our kingdom 's whole.
We thank you all, but most this Maid,

Who struck the gloom ablaze and led us here.
Name a bestowal speaking her desert,
And, if within our range, 't is hers.
You all must love her.

　　Al. Sire, if I may speak, she should be a duchess
In her own right, with broad domain.

　　Du. Give her England, Sire, she has half conquered it,
An' she 'll lead on, we 'll do the rest for sport.
They 've overstayed their time and it 's but fair
That we should lark with them.

　　K. Too fast, Dunois, she 's not a trespasser.

　　de B. I say, Sire, she should have what she choose herself.

　　K. Well spoke, de Baudricourt. What says La Hire?

　　La H. An' you could match her, Sire,
She 'd breed a race of warriors.

　　K. Ever an Armagnac! . . . Tremoille?

　　Tre. I can not judge in maids' matters.

　　K. You stay your counsel when she 's in debate
With shoulder shrug and elevated brow.
There is a hiss of envy on your tongue;
Beware the reptile sting you not; 't will kill.

　　Q. Yo. There is a hatch of treason in his heart
Which his o'er-stalking pride would fain let fly.
He 's ware with you, my Lord, to meet his aim
And venom all who near thee for thy good.
The Maid, I fear, is o'er the danger line.

　　Tre. If but a man would gall me with that speech!

　　La H. Her speech is mine to bellow in your ears
At dawn, at noon-tide, when you are asleep;
As humor pricks me or as chance may serve,
And if you dare to crook a joint at me,
Or give a look that might offend a king,
I 'll hew you shapely to the sexton's turn,
And spin you to him in death's gala dance.
Sleek, fawning greyhound; ingrate to the core!

　　Tre. If but this royal presence gave me leave

I 'd make this freebooter call back his words.

La H. If but,— but if. Leave, leave, my King, give leave!
I 'll cut his heart out!

K. Unhand your swords. What! in the presence of
Our scarce worn crown, ourself, our court,
This heaven-commissioned Maid?
Has France not wounds enough but you must draw?

Tre. My Lord —

K. Peace; not another word. I 'll not endure it.
I 'm too long patient.
Come, gentle Queen, speak you now for the Maid.

Q. Yo. From this fair presence let her choose a mate,
From those not mated, and name what dower she will.

K. That suits us best, a jewel in our court.
Joan, you have a princess' right.
Choose whom you will and you shall be endowered.

> [*Joan comes forward and kneels before the King.*

Joan. I fain would go to my own people
And do as I was wont.

K. You cast them off to do a mighty work,
Not yet fulfilled. The English still are here.

Joan. Obeying God, I came to crown you King
My task is done. Home clings now to my heart
And pulls me back. I pray you let me go.

K. We offer you the splendors of a court.

Joan. I was not born to it; let me go home.

K. Habit has made you stranger to it. What would you do?

Joan. Glad all their hearts; sew by my mother's side;
Tend flocks and go to church, as I was wont.

K. The voices that you heard would send you back
To finish up your work.

Joan. Then I would come.

K. Ask anything but that. You must not go.

Joan. Oh, Sire, but give me leave.
I 've known but duty since I saw the light.
Obedience to my God, my King, my home,

And love for all.   I was his instrument to do his will,
And now he leaves me to those blessed ties
Which make my world and happiness for me.
I pray you let them keep me, 't would make all whole
At home.   They take me back, I can not reason —
Only let me go.

 K.   It must not be.   Rest here awhile; talk with the Queen;
Consider more your state.   [*To the Queen.*]   She 's in
Your charge, entice her to our will.
My lords, the State requires our care,
We must to other council.

 Tre.   [*Aside to La Hire.*]   After the council in the outer court.
 La H.   Never sped minutes half so slow till then.
        [*Exeunt all but Queen and Joan.*

 Joan.   [*Aside.*]   La Hire means mischief; his eyes glare ruin
Hungry as death.   He knows no pity when his mood is so.
Blood, French or English, but it must be blood.
I 'll be beforehand with these desperate men.

 Q. Yo.   Come, gentle Maid, I 'll tell you what to do.
 Joan.   I pray you leave me here, I 'll tend you soon.
 Q. Yo.   Well, then, farewell; but come before you sleep.
             [*Exit.*

 Joan.   Oh God, have you deserted me?   Dear angel voices,
Whither have you gone?   Must I be stifled
In this whirl of power?   Oh, take me from this world,
My father's house no more.   Dear Domremy, the woods,
Haumette, good Father Philip.
Oh Riel, could thou but claim me now,
I 'd worship thee.

      Enter RIEL.

Oh Joan, Joan, thou art wretchedness!
 Riel.   Joan!
 Joan.   Whose voice is that?   [*Sees Riel and swoons in his arms.*
[*Awaking.*]   Oh Riel, am I in Domremy?

Riel.　You are with me, and that is all the world.

Joan.　Is this place not the King's?

Riel.　It is.

Joan.　How came you here?

Riel.　de Baudricourt staid me.

I fought with you where'er you went,

And am to-day made his page.

Joan.　I dreamed I saw you.

Riel.　'T was on the battlefield with Talbot.

I went to guard you praying, and feigned death.

Joan.　'T was heaven directed me.

What news from home?

Riel.　I know no more than you;

The King has ennobled you, made Domremy **tax free,**

And your brother Governor of Vaucouleurs.

Joan.　God bless him!

Riel.　This takes you farther from me.

Joan.　Nothing can do that but yourself —

Heard you what he said even now?

Riel.　Every word; he is ungrateful!

You must fly with me;

de Baudricourt knows all and will do all.

Joan.　Question him not, nor

Stir up mutiny within my heart,

Nor make temptation fight against my soul.

To fly is fear, and duty should not fear.

The day 's not wasted since the King was crowned.

If I discredit him 't will license all;

Then falls the work God gave into my hands

Through me, a rebel to my King and God.

Then speak no more of flight, but strengthen me,

Unguided in this wilderness of pomp.

Riel.　Then you do fear?

Joan.　Nothing but treachery, which all may fear.

One wish, dear to my heart, is unfulfilled,

I would deliver the good Duke Orleans,

Who has pined in English prisons since Agincourt,
Unransomed.   For that I 'll sue the King;
And now, farewell.   Be near me and stay with me,
'Till all is o'er, if it is ever o'er.
Once more, farewell !   I must to the Queen
And tell her I am endowered with love for you
To end dispute 'bout gifts and gratitude.   [*Exit.*

SCENE X.

Rheims.   Outer Court.

Enter LA HIRE *and* TREMOILLE.

Tre.   Now, villain, eat your boast or make it good.
La H.   It 's not my dinner time ; nor are
Your viands suited to my taste; but I have here a
Very grave discourse importing quietude
And cold respect, which my impatient blade
Would fain impart.
Tre.   How ill coarse wit becomes a dying man.
But die as you have lived, so falls the oak.
Come, base marauder, hell is gaping wide.
La H.   'T will get the hiccups when I toss you in.
Now, Maid of Orleans, you shall have revenge.
          [*They fight.   La Hire slightly wounds Tremoille.*
Exquisite pupil, this is my opening,
Now for the matter.   [*They fight again.*

Enter THERON.

The.   Hi, ii, hi, here 's a new war ; French against French !

My first adventure.   I 'll take a bout until this bout
Is fought, then claim the carnage as discoverer.
                    [*Exit.   Running against Joan, falls headlong.*

JOAN *rushes between* La Hire *and* Tremoille *and beats up*
                    their swords.

    Joan.   Hold! hold! my lords, for shame!
Is this the issue of our hard-won realm?
Must lillies blush for blood, not bloom in peace?
In God's name, lords, how could you do this thing?
Begone, Tremoille.   How dare you go behind the
King's command?   Begone, I say ;
'T is in his name I speak.   [*Exit Tremoille.*
And you, La Hire, I thought you better schooled.
    La H.   Why did you come between us?   He shall not 'scape
To coil about the throne and set his fangs in you.
    Joan.   Be ruled, be ruled ; he 's but a butterfly.

            Enter English Guards with French Prisoners.

What have we here?   Frenchmen in bonds coupled
Like felons for the market place !
Who are you, friends?
    1st Pris.   We are captives to the English.
    Joan.   Captives to the English !
Do all our victories but end in this?
[*To guard.*]   Release these men.   We have a King
To whom you 're subject now.
    Guard.   These men were taken by the chance of war,
And are not ransomed.   In the capitulation
They were not named.
    Joan.   Nor need be.   We gave you freedom
Not to take your spoil, but yourselves hence.
'T is impudence intolerable !   Go, get you gone !

You shall not have a man.   No, by my banner,
Not a single man!

Enter KING *and his train.*

My liege, here is some grave mistake,
Here are French prisoners in your very court —
Are you a King, and is this kingdom yours?
  K. Why, how is this?
  Guard. These are our captives ta'en in open war,
Not ransomed nor released by stipulation.
  K. Free them at once.   If there is aught to pay
We 'll satisfy the claim.
  Guard. Your majesty's commands shall be obeyed.
  K. Joan, you must not fail our banquet;
Nor you, La Hire.   [*Exeunt all but Joan and La Hire.*
  Joan. I have a sorry thing that I must tell you —

Enter JACQUES D'ARC, MADAME ROMEE, *Joan's Brother and Sister.*

  La H. Here 's more intrusion, we had best retire.
  Joan. Oh, God, I 'm blessed, how light and shadows meet!
                          [*She embraces each.*
Your blessing, father!
  d'Arc. I bless you, daughter, and all is forgiven.
You are the light of all our hearts and house.
  Joan. How are all at home?
  d'Arc. All well and long to see you.
  Joan. Haumette and good Father Philip?
  d'Arc. All well, and he is here.
  Joan. Then I shall see him.
  d'Arc. For that he came.
  Joan. [*To La H.*] These are my jewels that no court can
  La. H. You 're blest indeed. I 'll leave you now.   [match.
  Joan. Nay, stay, for I must speak.
[*To her folks.*] I am hindered now beyond desire and will.

Bestow yourselves, and I 'll be with you soon.
Then for a happy meet.   [*Exeunt all but Joan and La Hire.*

   La H.   Your cup of joy must now be full.

   Joan.   Yes, yes; but on beyond 't is horrible.
My sight grows dim and I am sick at heart.
The future is all black; I can not read it.

   La H.   Why, my brave girl, you have redeemed a realm.
Of course there 's nothing left so bright as that.
The future 's dark but in comparison.
Your crown is won and will endure for ever.

   Joan.   I want no crown, but only peace and rest.
I can not have it.   I have been warned
Of some most horrid work, and I the victim.
My voices leave me.   Black, black, black is all I see!
Oh, pray for me and help me if you can.

   La H.   Now, by the holy cross! —

   Joan.   Nay, you 'll offend again.

   La H.   Then by my baton! which I 'll make a cross;
If any fiend that cogs about this earth
Harms but one hair of thy abounding locks,
Save that it be in combat, open, fair,
And then should shamble off to Tartary,
I 'd hunt him through its jungles day and night,
And mawl him howling to his devil's den
To chatter thanks that he had 'scaped La Hire.

   Joan.   Your oath is vain, brave soldier, vain, vain, vain;
I have spoken.   Farewell, the Queen awaits me.
This is the very last time we shall meet,
Except 't is yonder, whither I must lead.
Adieu, adieu, adieu!   [*Exeunt.   La Hire gazes after her.*

Enter THERON, *timidly.*

   The.   Sodom and Gomorrah!   They 've eat each other up,
Harness and all; not enough left to stead an
Honest man.   Much less the ten that are not

To be found.   That Armagnac is as rapacious
As a Vosges wolf.   There 's too much valor on the road.
I 'd rob milkmaids of their biggins but that they
Have cattle that will butt.
I wish I knew of a barn that La Hire would not burn.
I 'd set up a rope walk and furnish gibbets for the
New realm.   Jacob and Laban!   I 'll tend old d'Arc's
Sheep and marry the Maid.   But there is that fellow
With more lives than a cat; in one of his nine lives
He 'll treat me to a cat o' nine tails.
Manna in the wilderness!   I see it, I 'll join
The Cardinal's crusade and rob the camp
While it 's at prayers.   May they pray, as did the Tishbite
For rain, seven years.   [*Exit.*

ACT III.

King's Palace, London.

Enter BEDFORD.

Bed. Our royal Alexander is no more.
He left his conquests incomplete, astray,
Like to a reaper who has felled the grain,
Leaving the sheaves ungarnered.
Poor, fickle France rebels,
And our wild lords, freed from restraint,
Now make her haggard with lean misery.
Ravage doth herald desolation,
While virtues pelted, hide them from the storm,
As zephyrs cuddle when the whirlwind sweeps.
Weak-purposed Burgundy is sour with spleen,
He grudges us the conquests we have made —
Still claiming more and more.
His father's murder prompts him to revenge,
While his French blood is rebel to the thought.
Then there 's that canker of a Queen, the Dauphin's
Mother, broods o'er our cause, a deadly cockatrice,
Fell with intents.   Till France is tamed our infant King
Is on the wildest sea that ever threatened shipwreck.

Enter SUFFOLK.

I thought you were in France.
    Suff. I come from France with presents such as these.
                                        [*Shows his wounds.*

Bed. How speeds our cause?

Suff. Like to a spavined nag on a bad road.
Salisbury is slain; Orleans is relieved;
Our soldiers killed or scattered.
The French at last have seen John Talbot's back.
Rude Biscay's coast takes on a Euxine squint,
Where Amazons are like to plant a realm.

Bed. Tame your discourse, and tell your horrors straight;
How Orleans was relieved; how Salisbury fell;
Why Talbot fled, what panic seized our men —
Your prate of Amazons, what does it mean?

Suff. It means, my lord, our army moving south
By easy conquests, summoned faint Orleans,
And had it gasping in a clutch of steel,
When from its gates there sallied forth a Maid
Clad in white armor, on a charger black,
With a fair banner streaming o'er her head,
Leading ten thousand Frenchmen, all transformed
From butter men to furious fighting fiends,
Who charged with blows, not uttering an oath,
And scattered us like blackbirds on the wing.
I crossed the fury as our forces met,
And had my pay in wounds. Her sword is lightning,
And in her arm a thunderbolt abides.
She is the direst gem that ever decked
The front of iron war; and as the cannon
Void their dreadful throats, her flashing sword
Waves onset to her men. Bastile on Bastile
Did she win from us, and made our remnant
Shelter in the woods. Myself saw Talbot
Scurry through the brush. Salisbury fell
Headless from a cannon shot.
This for her parle. Now, listen to the rest.
Ere we could gather, she stormed and took
Both Jargau and Beaugency, the first where I
Defended; and I am ransomed hence with this wild tale.

The gale of her success now courts weak Rheims,
Where she would turn the key on England's
Power, and crown the Dauphin Monarch of the Realm,
O'er-stepping thus our tinsel laggard war
As leaping thunder o'ergoes wisps from fens.
These are my horrors straight, are they enough ?
    Bed. If not o'ertold, the half would cloak our English
Channel black; ink o'er the chalky cliffs of Dover,
And begrime the souring downs of wild North Umberland.
This is the poisonest hatch of scolding strife.
Either you have flouted truth with monstrous speech
Or Mars and Otrere have been outdone
And Troy's dread ally was a vaporing shrew.
[*Aside.*] Now will York fume and now will Warwick itch,
While Somerset will stir the faggots up.
Duke Humphrey, you 're a fool, and your smirk wife,
To war on Burgundy and hinder us ;
Protector of a realm, you do n't protect.
My Uncle Winchester must bear the brunt.
His money and his crusade we must have
With all the church he carries in his robes.
The House of Lancaster has had a shake.
    Suff. You muse, my lord.
    Bed. Ah, yes ; I had forgot.
Whence and who is this she-wolf?
    Suff. A cow-girl from the borders of Lorraine.
She 's scant eighteen, and says she is from God ;
To me she seemed an Ate sprung from Hell,
With its scaped legions, battling for the earth ;
Though some released, say she wept o'er our dead,
And freed some prisoners for charity.
    Bed. How is she titled, and how warranted ?
    Suff. She 's called Joan of Arc, and Ark she 's deemed,
As precious as the shrine of Israel's hope
Incarnate, with assurance, faith and grace.
And thus enchanted to her soldiers' view,

FROM AN ENGRAVING BY J. C. BUTTRE

" *She courts the heady currents of the fight,*
As confident as Nereid mounts the waves."
—*Act III. Sc. I.*

She courts the heady currents of the fight,
As confident as Nereid mounts the waves,
Chasing war's dreadful clamors 'round the field.
Howe'er we marvel, thus she leads the French.

    Bed. Indeed, indeed, this is a sorry push.
The French, you say, swore not?

    Suff. Nay, not an oath; and save hard breathing
And the clash of steel, they gave
No earnest of their vengeful work.

    Bed. Then La Hire was not there?

    Suff. Oh, yes, my lord; but never swore an oath.
The Maid forbids it. He prayed, though.

    Bed. La Hire prayed and did not swear?

    Suff. 'T was a sort of blasphemy.

    Bed. How?

    Suff. He prayed that God would help him
That day, as he would help God if God were La Hire
And he were God.

    Bed. The sacrilegious brigand!

    Suff. And then he forced Jack Talbot from the trench
While Alencon whelmed Gledstane at the bridge.

    Bed. What did Dunois?

    Suff. He rode beside the Maid and hewed his way.

    Bed. Say you our force was scattered in the woods?

    Suff. So bad that Falstoff and Talbot
Could not find each other for a moon.

    Bed. 'T is a mad moil and hard to ravel out.
What says fair Burgundy; came you that way?

    Suff. I did, my lord; he 's fair and foul betimes.
Fair when we win, but cloudy when we lose.
He wants more money, and that your brother Humphrey
Give up to him both Holland and Hainault.

    Bed. The Cormorant! And Queen Isabel?

    Suff. She screams like a pelican, says she 'll to the wars
And have it out with the fair Maid,
Petticoat 'gainst petticoat. So men may rest, you see.

Bed.   No rest for England, Suffolk.   We 'll summon
The whole realm.   I must to France and take the King along.
   Suff.   And marry him to the Cow-girl?
That 's the way his father got his mother,
And got a slippery dowry for his pains,
While she now jigs to a Welsh piper.
   Bed.   Tut, tut, my lord ; she is our sovereign's mother.
   Suff.   I know she is, and sister to the Dauphin,
Whose mother casts suspect upon his blood.
   Bed.   My lord, my lord, this goes well nigh to treason.
   Suff.   To speak a doubt upon the Frenchman's blood,
Or say French wives are slippery?
If that be treason, treason 't is to breathe,
And if it is, my sword shall answer for it.
   Bed.   No more, my lord, this is unprofitable.
Go summon Winchester to meet me here.   [*Exit Suffolk.*
So breaks our party into quarrels,
With gnawing hints and low disparagement.
My father laid not his foundation sure,
And Harry built too largely for the base.
'T is Winchester and I must prop the house.

Re-enter SUFFOLK.

   Suff.   My lord, a courier scarce breathed brings news.
The Maid has o'ercome Talbot and Falstoff at Patay,
Ta'en Talbot prisoner, forced every town that
Did oppose, and to triumph whole, has crowned
The Dauphin.   She speeds, my lord, like Atalanta's
Sprite, with Victory a lapwing at her heels.
   Bed.   So one mischance upon another treads,
And more are huddling.
Go quick to Burgundy, tell him he shall have both
Holland and Hainault, the dower of Humphrey's wife —
And more, ten thousand crowns, if he 'll secure the Maid.
   Suff.   What would you do with her?   At such a price

The Dauphin can not pay the ransom back.

   Bed. Hark ye, my lord, Winchester is the Church
This side of Rome. The Church has power.
The Maid says she 's divine. If it 's divinity,
Then we are wrong. If it is witchcraft,
Then we know our course.

   Suff. You would not burn the girl ?

   Bed. The judgments of the Church must be fulfilled.

   Suff. The thought of it doth curdle every vein.
Witches ride not along the battle's front
To charm the chances of a desperate fight.
Her witchcraft is her courage and her worth,
Which in brave men should find fair courtesy.

   Bed. Even now you called her an escape from hell.

   Suff. And the French demons, in the self-same breath ;
Who ne'er till her were rated adversaries.
I did not fail to tell you how she wept
And freed our soldiers, Queen Philippa's grace.

   Bed. Suffolk, you have offended more than once.
Your flippant tongue makes you intolerant.

   Suff. I have offended only with the truth,
And that offense I 'll practice till I die.
Were I o'erpacked with words I could say more.

   Bed. Your stubbornness will take you to your end.

   Suff. And stubborn truth will vindicate my name.

   Bed. My lord, your stomach is too high !
Besides, you 're charged with weakness for the sex,
So let it end.

   Suff. Indeed, my stomach is too high !
For murdering women I am all too weak.
If you were so 't were better for the King,
Yourself, and all.

   Bed. I will no more.
Your conscience best hold parley with your head,
When 't is chopped off the council will break up.
See that it meet, for on the award hangs

Suffolk's brittle life.   Saw you the Cardinal ?

  Suff.   He awaits you in his study.

  Bed.   Go, my lord.   [*Exit.*

  Suff.   Humph! He'd call the headsman to try Suffolk's nerves;
Well, let him call, and call, and call.
Ere he 'll contrive against the valiant arm
That o'ercame him in the open field,
Or be a packhorse in the guilty work,
Proud Suffolk shall be parted limb from limb
And hung in gibbets o'er the busy Thames.
The Regent, his uncle, and his brother-in-law
Are apt at dicker.   Let them if they dare.
Greed and Ambition, both are filmy-eyed.
The crown is not secure on Henry's head,
York and the Nevilles are a busy set.
They have the baby King within their grip ;
The Protector and the Regent are awry ;
Besides, there is a growing discontent,
And chivalry may not be empty boast.
Here is a swirl that might whisk off a crown.
Proud Regent, look to it !   Vengeance is divine.
If you do light this game of fire
The ashes may fly back into your face
And cause a pother that will wreck a throne.

ACT IV.

SCENE I.

Burgundy.

Philip the Good in his cabinet the morning after his marriage.

Phil. In every way I 'm flouted and disgraced.
I am a Frenchman, yet in arms 'gainst France.
That 's poison to my blood.
My ally whets me to avenge my father's murder,
Plies me with bribes, but aims to compass all
When I am used, my life and dukedom.
I 'm barnacled with plots, chicane grins
In upon my marriage feast, afflicts my bed,
Turns blissful dreams to nightmares that affright —
When will this dreadful game of empire cease?

Enter QUEEN ISABEL.

Q. Is. You 're stirring early, Duke;
Methought bridegrooms were laggards
To the State?
    Phil. War kills honeymoons as care kills sleep.
    Q. Is. Helen and Paris did not find it so,
And Harry the Fifth entwined them in a crown.
Cupid and Mars have junketed ere now,
So that their bout with you is not so strange.
    Phil. I am on other matters.
    Q. Is. Other matters! The father of sixteen children,
And husband of twenty-seven wives,
With the wine running in the streets

At a fresh marriage, and yet on other matters?
A careful ruler makes a thrifty State,
But sure a household has some privilege.
Brides are not beakers to toss off like that.

Phil. I beg you leave me, I am much distressed.

Q. Is. But I must not leave you till I 've cured
Your heart. I have news for you.

Phil. I have too much already; here are letters
Intercepted between the Protector
And the Regent, plotting my death.

Q. Is. Sure, that 's advantage. This game is Pope Joan.
They 've shown their cards, now play with them and win.

Phil. You speak in riddles.

Q. Is. Why, you 're as stupid as a married man,—
Adam would starve before he found the fruit.

Phil. What mean you by that?

Q. Is. These English mastiffs can lick naught but blood.
Be thou the ferret and hunt out the eggs.

Phil. Still you are flying;
Pray come to the point.

Q. Is. Well, then, my news: Joan of Arc is taken.

Phil. Joan of Arc?

Q. Is. 'T is rumored so. John of Ligny hath her.
The fearful John, your vassal, who fears
His aunt, and somewhat too his wife,
But much more you, who hold his legacy in doubt.
Poor John of Ligny, your John of Ligny!
Your trembling tool, with a potter's crest,
That shred of the House of Luxemburg,
Enough to make two Judases at least.

Phil. Well, then?

Q. Is. Secure the Maid, for she is England's bane.
She 's made them scamper, and that 's witchcraft dire,—
Sharp, pardon-proof, judged by sour England's pride,—
For which they 'll make her body end in smoke,
And give a royal ransom for their pains,

If you but let them work their will on her.
And in the doing of that precious act
They 'll quench the Dauphin's charm and make a wound
Whose piteous gaze shall strike them mute with shame,
And tell a tale to start the careless world.

Phil. The Dauphin, thus deprived, gives France to them,
And then they 'll turn on me.

Q. Is. Will they? My daughter is the mother of their King.
To crown him they 'll come o 'er. The Maid's
Unconquered spirit is afoot, French stomachs
Will not bide their English beer.
Join you with us, we 'll fix their bounds in France;
If they o 'er step we 'll give them Haman's dance.

Phil. The Earl of Suffolk left here but this hour.
He brought me Bedford's hollow grant of
Holland and Hainault, but said nothing of the Maid.
Perhaps he knew nothing.

Q. Is. The Earl of Suffolk is not a broker.
Some pliant tool the Cardinal will find.
If the rumor 's true, you 'll be visited.

Enter a Page.

Page. Pierron Cauchon, Bishop of Beauvais, awaits.

Q. Is. All is confirmed, the Cardinal is working.
Ask him a round sum. Shall I remain?

Phil. It would much please me. [*To page.*] Attend him.
                                                    [*Exit page*

Enter CAUCHON.

Phil. We 're glad to see you, Bishop,
This is our cousin, Isabel of Bavaria.
The so-called Dauphin makes her homeless
And she abides with us. Come you from Rouen?

Cau. From the city of that name, but ruin

Stared at me where'er I came.

    Phil.   It's a sad time. I hope the English now are more secure

    Cau.   So they think, my Lord, and with your aid
They hope to end the war.

    Phil.   That they 've always had, but what new service
Can I render them?

    Cau.   Joan of Arc, now known as Maid of Orleans,
Has been taken in my diocese.
She is now in your vassal's, John of Ligny's,
Charge, and as Judge-ordinary of King Henry
I summon you to deliver her for trial.

    Phil.   If she is John of Ligny's prisoner of war,
I have not the right. He is entitled to her ransom.

    Cau.   I am provided for this difficulty,
Which, being raised, I am empowered by
Cardinal Winchester to give you ten thousand livres
For her, which is as much as the French
Are accustomed to give for a king or prince.

    Phil.   It 's a round sum, and if it 's in my power
I will deliver her. So tell the Cardinal.

    Cau.   I am much beholden to you. Farewell.   [*Exit.*

    Q. Is.   She will burn ; this Bishop will be her judge,
So now prepare. I will go write my daughter.
Mischief in every form is swarming in,—
We 'll mix in it and play off sin for sin.   [*Exeunt.*

T. CHENSWICK

MONUMENT OF JOAN OF ARC AT ROUEN

" And monuments arose mid shouts of Joy."
—*Act V. Sc. II.*

ACT V.

SCENE I.

Rouen.

JOAN *in Prison.*

Joan. A star through that scant loophole
Sends its rays like a kind visitor
To cheer me up. I do not think I 've slept a wink
To-night. Last night I dreamed I was in Domremy
With Haumette, and that we planned a festival
To feed the poor, asking advice of Father Philip.
Then the scene changed — mercy was gone.
In filed an eager throng, threatening, pitiless.
A pile there was, an impious sacrifice,
Then darkness fell.
Again it changed. Fair France was free,
And monuments arose mid shouts of joy.
I woke with streaming eyes,—
I dared not sleep again.
To-night the King's affairs lay heavy on me.
I must be now nineteen. It 's full two years
Since I rode to the war. I did not think I 'd last so long.
One year I 've been in prison, still fighting for the King.
I wonder when 't will end. It must be day,
The star has faded. Methinks I hear the carol
Of a bird ; how free it sounds.
Mischief loads the air. It 's coming—

Enter CAUCHON.

Cau. Peace be with you, Joan,
How have you been since Sunday?
   Joan. [*Raising her chains.*] You see, as well I might.
Lord Bishop, you are to blame for this.
   Cau. You are now prisoner to the English.
   Joan. Yes, I know I have been betrayed and sold to them.
The English will kill me. You should have kept me
In the Church's prisons, away from men-at-arms.
   Cau. I came to exhort you to prepare for your trial.
   Joan. I am ready; what am I charged with?
   Cau. Witchcraft.
   Joan. Is it witchcraft to overcome the English?
   Cau. Witchcraft is intercourse with evil spirits.
   Joan. None ever had power over me except my
Evil jailors, my tormentors in prison,
Who put chains on me. Who is to judge me?
   Cau. The Church. I am to be one of your judges.
   Joan. Who governs here?
   Cau. The Earl of Warwick has charge.
   Joan. Is he a churchman?
   Cau. He is keeper to King Henry.
   Joan. And me, too, whom he would not keep long.
   Cau. You should be contrite.
Will you submit to the Church?
   Joan. Yes, God first served.
   Cau. Will you say the Ave and Pater?
   Joan. Willingly, if my Lord Bishop will hear me confess.
   Cau. I can not witness for you.
   Joan. God and my conscience must do that;
Do you but your priestly office.
   Cau. I must refuse you. Will you take counsel?
   Joan. None that you will give. My counsel is my Lord,
I can not sanction my betrayal.
I see, my lord, your priestly robe

Is but an English frock. Have a care,
There is a Judge o'er all. I came from Him.
    Cau. Do you believe you are in a state of grace?
    Joan. If I am not, I pray Him receive me into it;
And if I am, I pray Him keep me so.
I should be the most wretched of beings
If I did not think I was.
    Cau. Pray God you are.
Come now to your trial.   *[Exeunt.*

SCENE II.

Rouen.

Inquisition. CAUCHON *presiding.*

JOAN *led in in chains.*

    Cau. What is your name?
    Joan. In the place where I was born,
They call me Jeanette; in France, Joan.
    Cau. How old are you?
    Joan. About nineteen years.
    Cau. You say voices from Heaven directed you
In what you have done. What did they say?
    Joan. Some things that are for the King's ears,
Not for yours. It was to me they gave the charge.
I am much more fearful of saying anything
That would displease them than I am of answering you.
    Cau. But, Joan, is God offended if one tells true things?
    Joan. I come from God ; dismiss me to Him,
I have naught to do here.
Some things I will not tell you.

Cau. Why was your standard borne at the Coronation
In the Church of Rheims rather than those
Of other Captains?

Joan. It had seen all the danger,
And it was only fair
That it should share the honor.

Cau. Was it right to attack Paris on the day
Of the nativity of our Lord?

Joan. I truly think it fitting to keep the festivity
Of our Lady every day.

Cau. Do St. Catherine and St. Margaret hate the English?

Joan. They love what our Lord loves, and hate what he hates.

Cau. Does God hate the English?

Joan. Of the love or hate God may bear the English
And what he does with their souls, I know nothing;
But I know they will be put forth out of France
With the exception of such as shall perish in it.

Cau. Do you think your King did well
In killing, or causing to be killed,
My Lord of Burgundy?

Joan. It was great pity for the realm of France,
But whatever might have been between them,
God sent me to aid the King of France.

Cau. Has it been revealed to you whether you will escape?

Joan. The saints told me I would be taken,
And to take all in good part,
And care not for my martyrdom.

Cau. Did you not say to the soldiers that standards
In imitation of yours would bring good luck?

Joan. No, I only said fall boldly upon the English,
And I fell upon them myself.

Cau. What was the impression of the people
Who kissed your feet, hands, and garments?

Joan. The poor came to me of their own free will
Because I had never done them any harm,
And had protected them as far as was in my power.

Cau. That will do. We will confer.

> [*The Judges whisper, then Cauchon rises*
> *and addresses Joan.*

Cau. Joan of Arc, this tribunal finds you
Guilty of blasphemy, heresy and sorcery,
And its sentence is, that you be
Burned at the stake, and that
Execution be immediate.

Joan. And am I then condemned, and must I die?
Bishop, I die through you, an English priest,
And not a priest of Rome.
Thou dost blaspheme thine office and thy faith,
The Church thou servest and God's holy name,
When thou dost say that Joan has blasphemed,
Or is a heretic, or sorceress; the woods of Domremy
Are better schooled, and shall discomfit all
Your carping work. Alas, will they treat me so horribly,
So cruelly !   [*Kneels to the Bishop.*
Oh, give me instant death — cut off my head,
And let mine eyeballs watch my spirit's flight
And smile my body to its sweet repose.
Rather seven times so than to be vanquished
By the biting flames, and tossed
And scoffed at by the bickering winds.
My blood is pure and never was defiled,
Then let my soul like honey-laden bees
From banks of flowers mount fragrant
To the welcome that awaits.
Your silence halts,   [*Rises.*
Then must I die the death, a martyr's agony?
Alas, if I had been in the prisons of the Church
To which I submitted, and if I had been guarded
By churchmen, and not by enemies,
It would not have befallen me thus miserably.
Oh, I appeal to God, the Great Judge,
Against the wrong, the injustice done me.

Where shall I be to-night?   Ah, by God's grace
I doubt not I shall be in Paradise.
Ah, Rouen, Rouen, art thou then to be
My last abode?   Much do I fear thou 'lt suffer
For my death. [*Kneels.*]   Oh, God, pardon all
My enemies,— the Bishop,— the English.
Remember the King and his realm ; have all
In thy keeping, and receive me into thy Kingdom.   [*Rises.*
I ask pardon of all and that all priests
Will say a mass for my soul.
Will some one bless me with a cross
For Christ's dear sake ?

> [*A soldier breaks a stick, makes and hands her one.*
>   *She kisses it and puts it in her bosom.*

To the Church, to the Church, Father Isambard ;
To the Church, bring a cross from the Church,
And hold it up that I may see it till sight is gone!

> [*Soldiers seize her.*

France! France! dear France!   God and the saints
Help me!   Oh, blessed Saviour, Mary, my voices, my voices —
I hear —" Fret not for thy martyrdom,
For thou shalt come at last to Paradise!"
Yes, my voices were from God,
My voices have not deceived me.

> [*As she is being borne away she utters the cry,*
>   *"Jesus, I come!"*

[*Darkness falls upon the scene. Her Martyrdom at the stake is thrown vividly on the canvas. It slowly gives place to her triumphal Equestrian Statue, surrounded by a throng of worshipers with up-turned faces. The Marseillaise chanted in the distance, swelling to high notes, which die slowly away until silence reigns. Curtain drops.*]

www.ingramcontent.com/pod-product-compliance
Lightning Source LLC
Chambersburg PA
CBHW032356020726
47499CB00008B/2773